Mandi the Clown

and the
HULA HOOP CIRCUS

by AMANDA
SYRYDA

This story
begins like so
MANY do:

a girl with a **DREAM**, and a hula hoop or two.

I'm **MANDI THE CLOWN**, colourful
and fun, always spreading smiles,
and hula hooping a ton!

I dream of a **CIRCUS** with all my favourite things!

Let's get this dream going, see what fun it brings.

First to find
animals and what
tricks they will do.

Come with me
my friends, off
to the ZOO!

Albert the **A**L**LIGA**T**O**R, shiny and green,

I know what he can do, run the slushie machine!

Miss Bailey Bunny, tiny and white, **POOF** she's gone, into the hat, out of sight!

Lion oh lion, big, strong and brave,
FIRE hula hoops for him,
this act we must save!

Elle the **ELEPHANT**, a magical cutie,

she'll be the ring leader, a dazzling beauty.

A barrel of monkeys, maybe **FIVE** or **SIX**,

to stand on each other's heads and do juggling **TRICKS!**

Two panda bear babies, and momma panda too, a flip flop **TRIO** in the big top very soon.

Gina the
GIRAFFE,
so tall
and
long,
twenty
hula
hoops
she
will
spin
for
one
full
song!

Animals, check! Now what more do we need?   Tasty treats of course, we have kids to feed!

Cotton candy is a M**UST**,
three flavours or more,
a circus is not a
circus without this
at the door.

Popcorn oh popcorn for miles   and miles,
at the Hula Hoop Circus we'll   have popcorn
in PILES.

We have all we need, it's practice time now.

Build our circus skills, from start to final bow.

OOPS, slips and falls do happen, it's true, practice to get better...

WOW

how exciting!

My dream is on its way.

After weeks and weeks
of practice, tomorrow
is grand opening day!

We hooped, hopped and flew, the show was a **SUCCES**S!

Children's smiles said it most, our happiness said the rest.

TRICKS, and hoops, and flying bears too, my circus dream came true because of each one of you.

Thank you all for
believing in
my dream.

Reach
for the
STARS,
they are
closer than
they seem.

Mandi the Clown and the Hula Hoop Circus
Copyright 2016 by Amanda Syryda

Illustrations by Simon Glassman

Visit HulaHoopCircus.ca for more information and event bookings.

Find @MandiTheClown and @HulaHoopCircus on Social Media.

Wholesale discounts for book orders are
available through Ingram Distributors.

Tellwell Talent
www.tellwell.ca

ISBN
Paperback: 978-1-77302-016-7
Hardcover: 978-1-77302-015-0

Printed in the USA
CPSIA information can be obtained
at www.ICGtesting.com
JSHW042018180224
57427JS00013B/156

9 781773 020167